Word List

Here is a list of words that might make it easier
to read this book. You'll find them in boldface
the first time they appear in the story.

Williamsburg	WIL-yuhmz-berg
colonial	kuh-LOH-nee-uhl
recognized	RE-kig-nyezd
Revolutionary	re-vuh-LOO-shuh-nair-ee
dismounted	dis-MOUNT-ed
raisins	RAY-zuhnz
occasion	uh-KAY-shun
ammunition	am-yuh-NI-shun
homespun	HOHM-spuhn
ingredients	in-GREE-dee-uhnts
distracted	di-STRAK-tid
herbs	erbz
comfortable	KUHM-fer-tuh-buhl

Barbie™

A Ride for Freedom

BARBIE and associated trademarks are owned by and used under
license from Mattel, Inc. © 1999 Mattel, Inc. All Rights Reserved.
Published by Grolier Books, a division of Grolier Enterprises, Inc.
Story by Victoria Saxon. Photo crew: Lee Katz, Lin Carlson,
Dave Bateman, Susan Cracraft, Robert Guillaume, and Judy Tsuno.
Produced by Bumpy Slide Books.
Printed in the United States of America.
ISBN: 0-7172-8856-0

GROLIER
B O O K S

"I just love October!" Barbie thought, stepping outside the country inn. The year was 1775, and Barbie was near the town of **Williamsburg,** Virginia. She was staying with Sarah Moore, an old family friend. Mrs. Moore was a widow. Her only son, Ethan, had left to join the **colonial** army. The army troops were fighting against the British soldiers, who were called the redcoats. Barbie was helping Mrs. Moore run her inn until Ethan returned.

Barbie breathed in the cool evening air. "Hello, Blaze!" she said softly to her horse as she entered the barn.

Blaze was dark brown with a long, white patch that stretched down his forehead. Barbie fed Blaze some hay. She petted him gently while he ate.

Suddenly the horse's ears went back.

"What's wrong?" Barbie asked.

Blaze stomped his hooves, and Barbie saw his eyes widen with fear. Just then, Barbie heard the familiar clatter of a wagon being pulled by a single horse. She looked out the barn door and saw a man nearing the inn. He wore a dark blue hat pulled low over his forehead.

The man was urging his horse to go faster, but Barbie could see that the old, white mare was tired. Finally the man guided the horse up to the barn where Barbie stood in the doorway. He leapt off the wagon and removed his hat.

"Ethan!" Barbie cried. She **recognized** the man as Mrs. Moore's son. "Are you all right?"

"For now," Ethan replied, looking over his

shoulder. "But you must help me. The British want to destroy all of our supplies. I have some hidden in this wagon to bring to our soldiers. But I'm afraid there are enemy soldiers following me."

Barbie quickly set to work. Though she could not fight in the **Revolutionary** War, she wanted to help as much as possible. Barbie believed in freedom for the American colonies. She asked Ethan to help her unhitch the white horse. Then the two dragged the heavy wagon into the barn.

"Let's cover the wagon with hay," Barbie said.

Ethan and Barbie worked swiftly. Suddenly Blaze began stomping his hooves again. Barbie put her finger to her lips, signaling Blaze to be quiet. She listened carefully and heard the sound of horses galloping toward them.

"That must be the enemy soldiers. Hide up in the loft," Barbie told Ethan. "And make sure you cover yourself with hay. I'll deal with them."

Barbie stepped outside to take care of Ethan's

mare. The horse was tired and thirsty. Barbie gave her a large bucket of water just as the soldiers appeared around a bend in the road.

"Redcoats!" Barbie whispered, pulling her shawl around her. The six men rode their horses right up to the barn. A soldier with red hair slid off his horse and approached Barbie.

"We're looking for a man with a wagon full of supplies," the soldier said. "Have you seen him?"

Barbie's heart was pounding, but she thought quickly. "The only two people I have seen today are my friend and her son," Barbie replied honestly.

The man looked behind Barbie toward the barn. Barbie held her breath. She was afraid the redcoats would try to look inside. Ethan didn't stand a chance against six British soldiers.

Barbie looked over at Ethan's mare. She hoped the redcoats wouldn't recognize her as Ethan's horse. "Would you like some water for your horses?" she asked the soldiers.

"Thank you," the redheaded soldier replied. Then the other soldiers **dismounted** and led their horses to drink, one by one, from the bucket. Barbie fetched another bucket while keeping a watchful eye on the men. The redheaded soldier was staring at Ethan's mare.

"She's a good old horse," the man said.

"Yes," Barbie agreed, putting a fresh bucket of water down for the other horses.

"But she looks tired," the soldier continued. "You must have taken her out for a long ride."

Barbie thought for a moment. Then she replied slowly, "She has worked hard today."

The British soldier looked closely at the white mare. Then he looked at Barbie. "You should be more careful," he said. "She's too old to be worked so hard."

Suddenly he turned and called to the others. "Let's move on. We want to catch this man before sundown."

5

Barbie watched the men climb back on their horses.

"Thank you for the water," the redheaded soldier said, looking down at Barbie. Then he tipped his hat and rode off with the other soldiers.

Barbie let out a deep breath as she watched them ride away. As soon as they were out of sight, she raced back to the barn to get Ethan.

Chapter Two

"Thank you, Barbie," Ethan said, climbing down from the loft. "I heard everything. You handled those redcoats wonderfully."

Ethan walked outside to his white mare and began to pet her. "You did well, too, Lizzie," he added softly.

It made Barbie happy to see that Ethan treated his horse well.

"Lizzie has had some water," Barbie said. "I'll give her some food and put her in the barn with Blaze. Why don't you go inside and see your mother?"

"Thanks, Barbie," Ethan said with a wide grin. "But I think she's coming to see me!"

Barbie looked up and saw Mrs. Moore standing in the doorway of the inn. Mrs. Moore had silver-gray hair. She was tall and thin, just like her son.

"Ethan?" she called out. "Is that you?"

Ethan ran straight across the dirt yard toward the inn. He gave his mother a long hug.

"It's good to see you," Ethan said. "It looks like Barbie has taken good care of you."

"Oh, yes, she has!" Mrs. Moore replied. "Now, come in the house. I'll fix you something to eat. I'll bet you haven't had a hot meal in weeks!"

Barbie smiled as she watched Mrs. Moore lead her son inside. Then she finished feeding the horses.

Later that evening, Barbie, Ethan, and Mrs. Moore sat down to supper together. Afterward, they enjoyed a delicious queen's cake for dessert.

It was made with butter,
sugar, eggs,
cinnamon, and
raisins. Mrs.
Moore had baked it
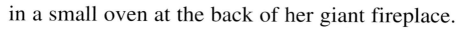
in a small oven at the back of her giant fireplace.

Ethan's face lit up when Mrs. Moore put
the cake on the table. "I thought I smelled your
queen's cake, Ma," he said. "This is a special
treat. I know how hard it is to get things like
spices, raisins, and sugar because of the war."

Mrs. Moore put her hand on her son's
shoulder. "It's a special **occasion**," she said to
Ethan. "You are safe and sound, and I don't have
to worry about you tonight. Let's enjoy our cake."

After they were finished eating, Ethan told
Barbie and Mrs. Moore that he would have to
leave soon. But first he would need to hide the
supplies that were in his wagon somewhere else.
He didn't want to risk his mother's and Barbie's

safety by keeping them in the barn.

"Right now the redcoats are looking for me and the supplies," he explained. "If I move the supplies, I will be able to go back and get them in a few weeks, when it's safer."

"How far do you have to go?" Barbie asked.

"About twelve miles," Ethan replied. "I just need to get to Yorktown. But I am worried about Lizzie. I'm afraid I wore her out today. I'm not sure she is strong enough for the trip."

Barbie also wondered if his old horse could make it. Lizzie was not as young as Blaze.

"Is there anything I can do to help?" Barbie asked.

"Well, yes, there is," Ethan answered eagerly. "Some of the merchants in the village have agreed to give us metals to melt down for **ammunition** to fight the British. I would go myself, but there is too much to carry on foot. And if I go with Lizzie, the two of us might be recognized."

"I can go on Blaze!" Barbie quickly replied.

"Thank you, Barbie," said Ethan. "The men who are giving us the metals will help you."

Early the next morning, Barbie looked out the window of her room on the second floor of the inn. The autumn sun was just beginning to rise. Its orange-yellow glow made the dew on her windowpane shine.

Barbie dressed quickly. Then she tiptoed down the creaky stairs, trying not to disturb Mrs. Moore.

When she got downstairs, she was surprised to see Ethan waiting for her. He had just finished putting some logs on the fire. Ethan told Barbie how to find the merchants. These fellow patriots would give Barbie the metals.

Barbie and Ethan headed out to the barn together. Blaze neighed as soon as he saw Barbie. He waited patiently while she put on his saddle.

Then Barbie mounted her horse.

"Don't worry, Ethan," Barbie said. "We will be back in no time." They said good-bye.

Then Barbie and Blaze galloped off down the road.

In town, Barbie found the men Ethan had described. They quickly loaded their bags of metal onto Blaze's strong back. They thanked Barbie and sent her on her way.

Barbie was very proud of Blaze. As they rounded the last corner to the inn, Barbie saw Mrs. Moore standing outside. She was watching Ethan work. He had uncovered his wagon and pulled it out of the barn. Lizzie stood nearby, drinking some water. Barbie slowed Blaze to a walk.

Ethan and Mrs. Moore looked up when they heard Barbie and Blaze approaching. They waved happily at them.

"Did you get everything?" Ethan asked.

"Yes, we did," Barbie replied, jumping down. "Thanks to Blaze, we had no trouble carrying the metals."

Ethan lifted up the heavy bags and put them in the wagon. Then he covered them with hay.

Ethan turned to hitch Lizzie up to the wagon. "I'm afraid she's limping today," he told Barbie. "Poor old Lizzie."

Barbie looked at the tired, old horse. Then she looked at her strong, young horse. She reached out and touched Ethan on the shoulder. "Wait," she said softly. "I think you should take Blaze instead." She handed Ethan the reins.

"But, Barbie, I can't take Blaze. You love that horse!" Ethan gasped.

"Yes, I do," Barbie said, feeding Blaze some hay. "So just make sure you both come back safely."

"I give you my word on that," Ethan said gratefully.

"And I'll take care of Lizzie," Barbie added

with a smile.

Barbie held onto Lizzie while Ethan hitched Blaze to the wagon.

Then, with tears in her eyes, Mrs. Moore bid her son good-bye. Ethan and Blaze headed down the road. Barbie squeezed Mrs. Moore's hand tightly. Then she quietly led Lizzie into the barn.

Chapter Three

Inside the barn, Barbie gently lifted one of Lizzie's feet. She wanted to see if she could figure out why Lizzie had been limping. Sure enough, Barbie discovered that Lizzie's hooves were badly worn.

"You're not too old, Lizzie," Barbie said. "We just need to give you a good rest and get you some decent shoes."

Barbie began cleaning Lizzie's hooves. She was determined to nurse the horse back to health.

After working on Lizzie for a while, Barbie went to find Mrs. Moore. She found the older woman outside, standing next to a barrel. The barrel was full of ashes. Beneath the barrel was a small metal tub.

"Are you making soap?" Barbie asked.

"That's right," Mrs. Moore replied. "Would you mind getting me some water while I start the fire?"

Barbie filled a bucket with water. She and Mrs. Moore slowly poured it over the ashes in the barrel. The water trickled through the ashes and dripped through tiny holes into the tub. Then the two women dragged the tub of ash water to the fire and added some cooking grease. They took turns stirring the mixture until soap formed.

"I wish I knew how I could help Ethan and the other colonial soldiers," Mrs. Moore said.

"Oh, I think you're helping a lot," Barbie told her. "Don't forget about all that cloth!"

Mrs. Moore had been making cloth for the soldiers. She would spin wool into thread on her spinning wheel. Then she would weave the thread into cloth on her loom. Many of the colonists had started making **homespun** clothes for the soldiers.

"In fact, I would like to help you make some more," Barbie said. "Our soldiers must get very cold camping outside at night."

"That's a wonderful idea, Barbie," said Mrs. Moore. "If you'll spin the wool, I'll weave it into cloth."

For the rest of the fall, Mrs. Moore and Barbie worked late every night making clothes for the soldiers. Barbie also tended to Lizzie in her spare time. Each day she got up extra early to feed and brush the old horse.

As Christmas approached, the weather got colder. Barbie and Mrs. Moore gathered holly and evergreen branches and bright red berries to decorate the inn. They also collected the **ingredients** they would need to bake Christmas holiday bread for their neighbors.

Barbie noticed that Mrs. Moore seemed **distracted.** Barbie knew she was thinking of Ethan and the other colonial soldiers who were spending the chilly nights outdoors. There would be no Christmas supper or warm fireplaces for them to enjoy this year.

One morning in December, Barbie went out to the barn to see to Lizzie. She checked Lizzie's hooves and petted the horse's mane. Barbie could tell that Lizzie was healthier and stronger. In fact, Barbie decided it was time for Lizzie to get some new shoes.

"Let's go visit the blacksmith!" Barbie said. The horse snorted and stomped her feet happily.

Barbie quickly got Lizzie ready. She put a saddle on her but decided not to ride her. Instead, she and Lizzie walked down the road into town.

Even the blacksmith commented on how healthy Lizzie seemed. Soon Lizzie had been fitted with new horseshoes. Then, as Barbie began to lead the mare back home, she stopped. "Are you ready, Lizzie?" Barbie whispered to her softly.

The horse neighed and tossed her head. Barbie hopped onto Lizzie's back. First the old horse began to walk. Then she began to trot. There was no sign of a limp at all as the white mare moved gracefully down the road.

"Good for you, Lizzie!" Barbie cried as they entered the barn. "I knew you could do it!"

Later that night, a man wearing a thin coat arrived at the inn. He was of medium height with thick, brown hair.

"Welcome," Mrs. Moore said as he walked in the front door. "Come sit by the fire. You look nearly frozen!"

"Thank you," the man replied gratefully. "My name is Tom. My friend Ken is outside tending to our horses. May we keep them in your barn for the night?"

"Of course," Mrs. Moore replied.

"I'll go help him," Barbie added. She quickly pulled on her warm coat and went out to the barn.

Ken was just leading the horses into the barn when he saw Barbie. Ken looked at Barbie and smiled. He saw kindness in her eyes. Barbie saw the same thing when she looked at him.

"Let me help you," Barbie said. She introduced herself. Then she and Ken fed the horses and made sure they were safe for the night.

While they worked, the two chatted about the war. Barbie soon learned that Ken was a patriot. He and Barbie both believed in freedom for the colonies. She wondered if he might even be a soldier.

Back inside the inn, Mrs. Moore had placed two warm bowls of hasty pudding on the table for Ken and Tom. The pudding was made with a mixture of cornmeal, water, and milk.

"I'm sorry we have nothing more to offer," Mrs. Moore apologized. "But at least this should warm you up."

"Thank you," Tom said gratefully. "It's the best hasty pudding I've ever tasted."

"The British have all the tea," Mrs. Moore began. "But Barbie has made her own tea from **herbs** she grew in the garden this year. Would you like to try a cup?"

"That would be wonderful," Ken replied.

Barbie put a kettle of water on the fire.

"Have you any news about the war?" Mrs. Moore asked.

"Well, I'm sure you've heard about the British governor," Tom replied. "We managed to drive him out of his house and onto one of the British ships. Right now, he and his men are floating outside the town of Norfolk." Tom chuckled at the thought of the governor sitting out on his ship with no way to land on shore.

"I'm afraid he might shoot his cannons from the ship and attack the city," Ken said quietly. Tom frowned and nodded.

A silence crept into the room as all four of them thought about the seriousness of the war. Barbie shivered. She and Mrs. Moore were very worried about young Ethan. Barbie also wondered if Ken and Tom might be in danger as well.

"Well," Mrs. Moore said suddenly, "is the water ready yet, Barbie?"

Barbie nodded and quickly poured the boiling water over the dried herbs. Minutes later, the tea was ready. Both Ken and Tom said how good it tasted. Barbie was happy to see that the men had finally warmed up.

After talking a bit more, Mrs. Moore led Ken and Tom upstairs to their rooms.

When Barbie stood up to clean off the table, she saw that Tom had left his scarf on the bench. Barbie picked up the scarf, thinking she would hang it up by the fireplace. She noticed that it had a large hole. She knew that Tom would need it to keep warm the next day. So she immediately set to work mending the scarf.

As she worked, Barbie listened to the cold winter wind blowing outside. It didn't take her long to finish the mending. She thought about Ken out in the cold. Like Tom's, his coat was thin. Without a second thought, Barbie picked up the

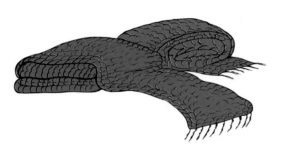 scarf she had been making for Ethan. She sat back down and began to knit.

To finish, Barbie worked late into the night. "I'll make another scarf for Ethan later," Barbie thought. "Right now, Ken needs this more."

Chapter Four

Late the next morning, Barbie awakened to the sounds of laughter downstairs. She got dressed and hurried to the kitchen. There, she found Ken and Tom sitting at the table. They were enjoying a special breakfast of cornmeal pancakes called johnnycakes.

Mrs. Moore was telling the men how difficult it was to sew because of the war. "We can't get any pins!" she exclaimed with a chuckle. "We've tried every kind of replacement we can think of. Why, I've even tried using thorns!"

Ken and Tom were laughing as Barbie

entered the room.

"Good morning, Barbie!" the men said.

"Good morning," answered Barbie.

"Would you like to sit down?" Ken offered.

"No, thanks, Ken," Barbie replied. Then she
turned to Tom. "You left this downstairs last
night," she said, handing him his scarf.

"Thank you," Tom said. "Oh, look, you've
mended it!"

"I didn't want you to be cold on your trip,"
Barbie said.

Then Barbie handed Ken the other scarf
she had made. "This one is for you, Ken. I noticed
you didn't have any scarf at all. Merry Christmas,"
she said.

Ken looked surprised, but he took the scarf
and smiled gratefully. "It's beautiful, Barbie," he
said. "Thank you."

After breakfast, Ken and Tom went out to
the barn to saddle up their horses. Barbie helped

them. Then she waved as they rode out of sight. She was glad to know they would be warm. She only hoped they would be safe, too.

For the rest of the morning, Mrs. Moore and Barbie baked holiday bread. It was the day before Christmas Eve. They planned to give the bread as gifts to their neighbors.

That afternoon, Barbie and Mrs. Moore set out early to deliver the bread. They decided to cut through a wooded area at the edge of a nearby farm. Walking under some large beech trees, Barbie listened to the dry leaves crunching under her feet.

She breathed in deeply. She loved walking in the crisp, winter air. For a moment, Barbie almost forgot about the war.

Suddenly Mrs. Moore grabbed Barbie's arm

and put her finger to her lips. Then she pointed to something in the distance.

Barbie could barely make out a strange shape leaning against the bottom of a tree. Looking again, she saw that it was a man.

"He looks like he's hurt!" Barbie gasped.

"Yes, he does," Mrs. Moore whispered. "But what if he's a British soldier? Perhaps we should go get help."

Barbie was about to agree when she noticed something familiar about the man. He was wearing the scarf Barbie had made.

"It's Ken!" she exclaimed, racing over to him.

"I'm so lucky you came this way," Ken said as soon as he saw Barbie and Mrs. Moore. "I'm hurt. I can't walk."

"Where's Tom?" Barbie asked.

"We got separated back there on the road," Ken replied quickly.

Barbie turned to Mrs. Moore. "Can you stay

here with Ken?" she asked. "I'm going to run home and get Lizzie!"

"Of course," Mrs. Moore replied. "And be careful, Barbie!"

Chapter Five

Barbie raced back to the inn as fast as she could.

"Come on, Lizzie," she whispered as she saddled her up. "We need your help."

Barbie knew that Lizzie's hooves were better. But were they ready for a hard ride? Barbie climbed onto Lizzie's back.

"You can do it, Lizzie," Barbie said. "I know you can."

Barbie urged the horse forward. Lizzie whinnied and started to gallop. Barbie smiled. She could tell that Lizzie was completely healed.

Barbie guided the horse along the road and into the woods. In no time at all, they had reached Mrs. Moore and Ken.

"That was fast!" Ken exclaimed. He tried to smile, but Barbie could tell that he was in pain. Ken struggled to get to his feet.

Barbie and Mrs. Moore rushed to his side. Then they helped him up onto Lizzie's back. The horse carried him back to the inn, with Mrs. Moore and Barbie walking alongside.

After helping Ken into one of the rooms off the kitchen, Barbie rode into the village to get the doctor.

"There's nothing you can do except try to make him **comfortable,**" the doctor said after he had bandaged Ken's ankle.

"But I have to leave right away," Ken said.

"I'm afraid you shouldn't do any walking at all for at least a couple of weeks," the doctor replied. "You've got a broken ankle."

"If I could get a horse," Ken began, "would it be all right for me to ride?"

"No," the doctor said firmly. "Just rest here and let Barbie and Mrs. Moore take care of you. You're in good hands."

Ken sank back against the pillows on his bed. Barbie could tell he was disappointed.

"Thank you, Doctor," Barbie said as she and Mrs. Moore walked him to the door.

When she returned to Ken's room, Barbie found him trying to get up and walk.

"Ken!" Barbie cried. "What are you doing?"

"I'm sorry, Barbie," he said. "I can't explain. I just need to leave. I have to be somewhere."

Barbie sighed. "Just sit down for a minute and talk to me. What's really going on?"

Ken sat on the bed and looked at Barbie. "All right," he said. "My horse threw me this morning while I was riding through the woods. Then she ran off. That's when you found me."

Barbie nodded as Mrs. Moore walked into the room. "What else?" Barbie asked. "You can trust us."

Ken smiled. "I know I can. I was just worried that I might be putting you in danger. Here's the truth. Tom and I are colonial soldiers. We were sent to Virginia by General Washington. He wanted us to collect some supplies for our troops. A couple of months ago, several of our soldiers hid some supplies near Yorktown. They wanted to keep the British troops from stealing them."

Barbie gasped. "You must be talking about the supplies that Ethan hid."

Ken looked at Barbie and Mrs. Moore. "That's right," he said. "Tom and I were supposed to meet Ethan today. We planned to wait together until tomorrow night, Christmas Eve. Then we would gather the supplies while everyone was sleeping. When we left your inn this morning,

Tom went straight toward Yorktown. But I had some business in Williamsburg. There I learned that the redcoats had found out about our plan. I raced away to catch up with Tom and Ethan."

"Is that when your horse threw you?" Barbie asked.

"Yes," Ken replied. "Now I fear that British soldiers will be waiting for Tom and Ethan tomorrow when they arrive in Yorktown. Then Tom and Ethan could be attacked!"

"Oh, no!" Mrs. Moore cried. For a moment, everyone was silent. Finally the older woman spoke up. "How can we help?" she asked.

"I have an idea," Barbie answered slowly. "I'll ride Lizzie to warn Ethan and Tom. Can you tell me exactly where they are, Ken?"

"Yes," Ken replied. "Are you sure you want to do this?"

"What about Lizzie?" asked Mrs. Moore. "Isn't she too old?"

Barbie looked at her two friends. "I want to do this," she said with confidence. "And I'm sure Lizzie can do it, too."

Ken smiled. Then Barbie spoke again. "Now tell me how I can find Ethan and Tom. I'll leave first thing in the morning."

Chapter Six

As the sun was rising the next morning, Barbie saddled up Lizzie. She was about to leave when she heard a voice call out.

"Wait!" Mrs. Moore shouted from the doorway of the inn. "You forgot something."

Mrs. Moore ran over and handed Barbie a large bundle. "It's some of the clothes we've made. Please make sure Ethan keeps a coat for himself."

"Thank you, Mrs. Moore," Barbie said. "I'll do that."

Mrs. Moore took Barbie's hand. "And take

care of yourself, dear."

"I will," Barbie answered. Then she tied the bundle to Lizzie's saddle and rode off.

Barbie let Lizzie go as fast as she dared over the dirt road.

Finally, by late morning, Barbie reached a bend in the road. She stopped at a nearby stream to get some water for Lizzie and herself. Barbie looked at the sun in the sky and realized she did not have much time left to catch up with Ethan and Tom. They were meeting other colonial soldiers in a secret cellar at the Eagle Tavern. If she did not reach them in time, then they might leave and be captured by the British soldiers.

Barbie knew that if she cut through the woods to the left, she could get to the tavern much faster. But the road to the right was smoother and would be easier for Lizzie.

Barbie quickly made her decision. She dismounted and led Lizzie through the woods to

the left. Lizzie did well at first. She scrambled through the rough brush and stepped surefootedly over fallen logs. But when they reached a small hill, Lizzie stumbled and nearly tripped over some rocks.

"Come on, Girl," Barbie whispered in Lizzie's ear. "You can do it. I know you can."

Lizzie nuzzled Barbie's hand with her nose. Then the horse followed her faithfully through the heavy brush up the hill.

When they reached the top, Barbie climbed back onto Lizzie's back. They began to race through the woods.

At last, Barbie saw a clearing. It was the road leading to the tavern.

Suddenly Barbie heard the noise of horses galloping down the road. She tried to hide herself and Lizzie behind some trees, but it was too late. Before she knew it, Barbie saw the bright red coats of two British soldiers.

The soldiers stopped as soon as they saw Barbie.

"Where are you going, and what is your business?" one of the soldiers called out to her.

Barbie took a deep breath. "I'm just on my way to visit some friends in Yorktown," she said as bravely as she could.

The soldier moved closer to Barbie. Then suddenly his face broke into a wide smile.

"I know you!" he exclaimed. "We met at your inn near Williamsburg."

Barbie recognized the redheaded soldier. He had stopped at the inn the day Ethan had returned.

"Well, you must be telling the truth," he said with a laugh. "You can't travel very far with that old horse."

Then the man turned to the other soldier. "Come on, let's go," he said.

Barbie sighed with relief as she watched them ride out of sight.

"That was a close one, Lizzie," she said, patting the faithful horse.

A few minutes later, Barbie arrived at the Eagle Tavern. She slid off Lizzie and looked around, wondering how to find the hidden cellar.

Suddenly she felt someone tap her on the shoulder. It was Ethan, and Tom was with him!

"I need to talk to you," Barbie said quickly. Then she gave the men the message from Ken. When she was through, she handed them the clothing.

"The soldiers in Boston will certainly appreciate these," Tom said.

"There's a warm coat in there that your mother would like you to keep," Barbie told Ethan.

"Thank you, Barbie," Ethan replied. Then he turned to Lizzie. "Good old Lizzie."

"Yes," Barbie agreed. "She brought me all the way here from Williamsburg!"

Ethan looked at his horse in amazement. "Would you like to see Blaze?" he asked Barbie.

Barbie nodded eagerly. As soon as the three reached the woods behind the barn, Barbie heard Blaze's familiar whinny.

"He's happy to see you!" Tom exclaimed.

Barbie was relieved to see that Blaze was still healthy and strong. She stroked his neck.

"He's helped me a lot over these past few months," Ethan told Barbie.

"Lizzie's helped me a lot, too," Barbie replied softly.

"Will you be all right traveling home by yourself?" Tom asked Barbie, frowning.

"I'll be fine," Barbie said. "I have a good horse to guide me."

The two men thanked Barbie again.

Then Barbie and Lizzie began the long

ride back home.

As she rode, Barbie smelled smoke coming from the chimney of a nearby farmhouse. Inside she could see a family setting the table for their Christmas Eve supper. Some sprigs of holly had been placed in the window for decoration. Barbie smiled. Then she urged Lizzie to gallop a little faster.

Chapter Seven

The next morning was Christmas Day.

Barbie was glad to awaken safely in her warm bed at the inn.

Barbie sat up and looked out her window. A thick blanket of snow had fallen during the night and covered the countryside.

"It's beautiful!" she said to herself. "What a wonderful Christmas surprise!"

Barbie didn't know it, but there was another surprise waiting for her.

As she looked outside, she saw something move near the barn. When she looked closely,

Barbie saw Ethan holding Blaze by the reins! Mrs. Moore was standing outside, talking to her son.

Barbie jumped out of bed, got dressed, and ran downstairs. When she stepped outside, she saw Mrs. Moore leading Blaze to the barn. Ethan was gone.

"Mrs. Moore!" Barbie called, running toward her through the snow. "Where's Ethan?"

"Everyone is safe," Mrs. Moore explained. "He and Tom were able to move the supplies during the night without any trouble."

"Thank goodness!" Barbie said with relief. "But why did Ethan leave without Blaze?"

"The British soldiers know about Ethan," Mrs. Moore explained. "They are searching for a man riding a brown horse with a white marking on his forehead. Tom told Ethan to bring Blaze back here and then walk to a farm a couple of miles north. Without Blaze, Ethan won't be recognized by the British soldiers. Tom found

Ken's horse. Now it's waiting for Ethan at the farm."

Barbie reached for Blaze, who nuzzled her cheek. "I'm glad to hear Ethan is safe," she said. "And I'm glad Blaze is safe, too."

Later that afternoon, Mrs. Moore and Barbie prepared a special Christmas dinner for themselves and Ken.

When they had finished eating, they exchanged gifts. Barbie gave Mrs. Moore a hat she had made from their homespun cloth, and Mrs. Moore gave Barbie a warm cape.

Then Ken handed a small packet to Mrs. Moore. "I'm afraid it's not much," he said. "Luckily, I was able to find these in town just after we left your inn. I didn't know when I would see you again, but I wanted to get them for you anyway. Who knew I would be seeing you again so soon!"

Mrs. Moore opened the package. Her face

lit up. "Pins!" she exclaimed. "Oh, thank you, Ken! These will be much better than thorns!"

Everyone laughed.

Then Ken handed another small packet to Barbie. Inside, there was a small silver charm in the shape of a horse.

Barbie's eyes shone as she looked at his gift.

"It's beautiful," she said softly.

Ken smiled. "You and Mrs. Moore have been so kind to me," he said. "Thank you for letting me join you for the holiday."

"Next year I'll make you a fine new shirt for Christmas, Ken," Mrs. Moore said with a wink. "Now that I have pins!"

All three friends laughed out loud.

Then they settled down with some hot herbal tea and enjoyed the rest of the evening together.

Barbie, Ken, and Mrs. Moore were very grateful for one another's company. They hoped this would be the first of many Christmases they would spend together when the war was over at last.